To the keeper of this book—it's time
for you to visit the magical kingdom
waiting within. Believe in yourself—that
will give you wings to fly!

To Elena Garrett, wonderful school librarian
at St John's School, Canterbury, and to all
school librarians everywhere.

OXFORD
UNIVERSITY PRESS

Great Clarendon Street, Oxford OX2 6DP
Oxford University Press is a department of the University of Oxford.
It furthers the University's objective of excellence in research, scholarship,
and education by publishing worldwide. Oxford is a registered trade mark of
Oxford University Press in the UK and in certain other countries

Text copyright © Anne Booth 2019
Illustrations copyright © Rosie Butcher 2019
The moral rights of the author have been asserted
Database right Oxford University Press (maker)

First published 2019

British Library Cataloguing in Publication Data

Data available

ISBN: 978-0-19-276625-0

1 3 5 7 9 10 8 6 4 2

Printed in India
Paper used in the production of this book is a natural,
recyclable product made from wood grown in sustainable forests.
The manufacturing process conforms to the environmental
regulations of the country of origin.

5 reasons why we think you'll love this book

Join Maya as she flies through the air to save the day

Meet the beautiful birds of the kingdom and their fairy friends

The natural world is full of wonder—turn to the back for fascinating facts!

Meet the fairy-wrens. They're splendid!

Colourin~ ~ ~ ~ ~ been ~ ~ ~ ~ ~ ~

Magical kingdom of Birds

The Missing Fairy-Wrens

ANNE BOOTH
Illustrated by Rosie Butcher

OXFORD
UNIVERSITY PRESS

Chapter One

'You're so good at swimming!' said Maya's friend, Saffron, to her.

'How do you swim so fast?' said Theo, Saffron's brother.

Maya, Theo, and Saffron were drinking hot chocolate together at Saffron and Theo's house after going swimming together. They were new neighbours and went to Maya's school, and all three had quickly become the best of friends.

'I've just done a lot of swimming, that's all,' said Maya. 'It helps my legs get stronger—it's so much easier for me to swim than walk really—my legs don't get as tired in the water.'

'And you are so good at horse riding too!' said Theo. 'I wish I could ride like you.'

'I'll take you next time,' said Maya, smiling at them. 'Penny and Dad said I should invite you to come with us to thank you for today. I'm so glad you've moved opposite me.'

'We're glad too!' said Saffron, beaming.

'So are you warmed up now after swimming?' said Emma, Saffron and Theo's mum. 'Is it a good time for me to teach you how to make paper flowers?'

Theo took the dirty cups out to the kitchen and brought three clean cups back. Then his mum, Emma, put out lots of lovely coloured paper onto the table. She showed them how to make a circle by drawing around a cup, and then she cut it out. Next she demonstrated how to cut a spiral in a circle, and then roll it

around a pencil, so they each had made
a beautiful rose.

'Thanks, Mum!' said Saffron. Emma
left them to it, as the three friends made
more and more flowers.

'I'm going to give some to our aunty for her birthday,' said Theo.

'I'm going to do that too,' said Saffron.

'Do you think I could make a bunch of them for Penny and Dad?' said Maya, as she finished making a rose. 'It's their wedding anniversary tomorrow. My big sister Lauren is coming back from university as a surprise and we are making a special meal for them, but I'd like to decorate the room too. I want them to feel special.'

'That's a great idea!' Theo said. 'I'll go and ask Mum for some more sheets of coloured paper for you to take home.'

'You can put them in the lovely satchel your mum gave you,' Saffron added, giving Maya a hug, as Theo came back with a big pile of coloured paper.

Maya had brought the satchel her mum had given her over to show Saffron and Theo. She couldn't remember her mum—Penny was her lovely stepmum—so it meant a lot to have had this satchel as a present from her. She was very proud of it and wanted to show her new friends. She hadn't told them about the magic colouring book and pencils her mum had put in the bag though—she had left them on her desk at home.

It was a little difficult to explain to Saffron and Theo that she wasn't just their school friend, Maya, she was also the Keeper of a magic book. When she was needed by her friends, Princess Willow, the fairy, and Patch, the talking magpie, a new picture would appear in the colouring book, and when she coloured it in she would be transported to the Magical Kingdom of Birds.

Maya said goodbye to her new friends and went back home. She hung the satchel over the back of her chair in her bedroom. Maya looked wistfully at the closed book on her desk. It had such a beautiful cover of deep-blue cloth, with lots of scenes of tiny gold birds flying, nesting, soaring, swooping in all sorts of places, all over it. In gold lettering on the front were the words *Magical Kingdom of Birds*.

'I wonder how Patch and Willow are,' Maya said out loud. 'I love my new friends, Saffron and Theo, but I miss Patch and Willow.' She had opened the book every day but there hadn't been a new page for a while, and without a page to colour in she couldn't get back to the kingdom to see her old friends.

She sat down and opened the satchel and took out the big wad of coloured paper Theo had given her to put inside. He and Saffron were so generous.

'I wonder if I could make some of the flowers I have seen in the Magical Kingdom of Birds?' she said. 'Even if there are no new pictures, at least I can look at the old ones I coloured in to give me some ideas. The flowers in the kingdom are so beautiful.'

As she reached to open the book to check the flowers she had coloured in before, she caught sight of a magpie hopping in the garden just outside her window. Every time she saw a magpie she thought of Patch, her friend. Maya felt a tingle of excitement when this one stopped and put his head on one side to look at her. He seemed to know her.

She opened the beautiful book to look at the pictures she had already done, but her heart started beating faster when she saw the book turn to a new page at last.

'They are calling me!' she said, and

looked for her pencils. 'Hooray! Hold on, Princess Willow and Patch—I'm colouring in the new page now! See you in the Magical Kingdom of Birds!'

Chapter Two

First a black, then a grey, a white, and finally a blue magic pencil rolled to Maya's fingers and helped her colour in the beautiful bird on the new page.

As she finished, the room began to spin around her. Maya wasn't scared as she was lifted into the air—she just felt really happy and excited. Glittering spirals of blue feathers flew around her, and she had the sensation that she was falling into the book. Maya knew this meant that her friends, Willow and Patch, needed her and that she was going back to the Magical Kingdom of Birds!

'Maya! How lovely to see you!' said fairy princess Willow. Maya was sitting in a garden full of flowering shrubs, and she found she was wearing her satchel over her shoulder. The sky was blue and it was warm and sunny. Willow was wearing a pretty dress made of leaves and a lovely flower garland crown which looked so striking against her black curls.

Willow and Maya gave each other a big hug.

'I'm so happy to see you, Maya!' said Willow. 'I can show you the Magical Kingdom in the spring! It has been so lovely seeing the spring come and not feeling cold any more.'

There was a beating of wings, and Patch the magpie swooped down and landed next to them.

'Hello, Maya!' he said. 'What adventure will the book bring us today?' His glossy black and white feathers gleamed in the spring sunshine. In the Magical Kingdom,

Maya was the size of Willow the fairy, and rode on Patch's back for adventures—it was so exciting soaring into the air with him.

Maya opened the book to show Willow and Patch the new picture.

'That's a male superb fairy-wren!' said Patch.

'What a lovely name!' said Maya.

'Actually, it's a superb name,' laughed Willow. 'And I think the book is sending us on an adventure with them. We will put the harness on Patch, and I will get your quiver of sticks, and then we will be off!'

Willow passed Maya a quiver with two beautiful hooked woven sticks she had made for her. Maya's legs were not very strong, and the sticks helped if she needed to walk, but mostly Maya used them to help get her and Patch and Willow out of tricky situations. The Kingdom of Birds was really all about flying, not walking, and Maya spent most of her time soaring in the air on Patch's back. With the quiver of sticks over her shoulder, her satchel and the book, and her two magical friends with her, Maya felt ready for any adventure!

Taking off from the ground with Patch was always exciting. Maya got on his back and he bowed and then rose into the air, extending his wings and rising as he beat them. Willow fluttered up beside them.

'Maybe the book just wanted you to see the Kingdom of Birds in spring,' said Willow. 'It's such a lovely time to visit the fairy-wrens. The feathers of the male fairy-wrens have turned from brown to gorgeous colours. The male superb and splendid fairy-wrens have turned blue!'

'So there are splendid fairy-wrens

too?' laughed Maya. 'What great names!'

'I think it's all a bit silly and show-offy,' said Patch, a bit crossly.

'There are eleven types of fairy-wren,' said Willow. 'But this picture is of a superb one, so they are the ones we will visit. It's such a pretty time to see them, as they will be picking yellow flower petals to present to female fairy-wrens they are interested in. We might see some blue splendid fairy-wrens too, and if we do, they will be picking pink or purple flowers.'

'Why do they choose those colours?'

asked Maya.

'Because they think they look good against their blue plumage,' snorted Patch scornfully, as they flew on over green forests and rivers sparkling in the sunlight.

'Well, I think it sounds very romantic,' said Maya. Her dad liked to buy flowers for Penny, but she didn't think he had ever tried to match them with his clothes. *Maybe I'll tell Dad to buy Penny yellow flowers to go with his blue shirt,* thought Maya, smiling.

As they flew through the Kingdom of

Birds, Maya could see that everywhere there was love in the air, with lots of boy birds showing off in front of girl birds. Male peacocks shook their wings and spread and rattled their shimmering tail feathers at peahens, and made very loud, shrill cries.

'They do make a racket!' complained Patch, as Willow flew down to them. 'Why do we have to go any nearer? They aren't songbirds, that's for sure.' He reluctantly swooped down so that Maya and he could join the princess.

'Hello, peacocks,' said Willow, hovering in the air above them. 'You are looking beautiful today, as always!'

'Thank you!' they said, as they strutted up and down, the markings on their long tail feathers making it look as if there were lots of eyes staring at all of them. 'Do you like our tail feathers, Princess Willow?'

'Of course! I think they are magnificent,' said Princess Willow, touching her flower garland as she spoke.

'Your new garland is exquisite, Princess Willow,' said a pretty little peahen. Her neck was the same blue as the peacocks, but the feathers on her body were brown and grey, and she did not have any long tail feathers. Her little head feathers shook as she spoke, so she looked as though she had a very delicate hat.

'Why, thank you,' said Princess Willow, looking pleased, and they flew on.

'Do you know,' said Willow, proudly. 'I don't think that the book brought you back to the Kingdom of Birds because there is a problem. I think it is just so that you can see how everything in the kingdom looks so lovely.' She adjusted her flowery crown as she spoke.

'Not everyone looks lovely. Look over there at those silly frigate birds,' snorted Patch. 'They puff out their red throats to impress the females. Why do they have to have red around their necks—what's wrong with smart black and white?'

'My dad wears a red tie often,' laughed Maya. 'Maybe he has the same idea! The Kingdom of Birds is so colourful! I think those birds look amazing!'

'Huh!' said Patch, a bit huffily. 'It's a bit

ridiculous if you ask me. I don't change the colour of my feathers at different times of year, or show off like that.'

Maya leant forward and gave Patch a quick hug round his smooth, warm, feathery neck.

'Why did you do that?' he asked, suspiciously.

'Don't worry. Everyone knows that black and white are the smartest colours of all, and that you look handsome all year round,' said Maya. 'You're splendid and superb all at the same time. You're my Magnificent Magpie!'

Patch gave a magpie chuckle.

'Hold on tight to your satchel and quiver!' he said, and suddenly started soaring and swooping down and up, so that Maya felt like she was on a roller coaster and laughed and screamed with delight.

'Patch and Maya! What on earth are you doing?' said Willow, a little crossly, as she had had to move quickly out of the way to dodge them.

'Just showing off, like all the birds are doing,' laughed Maya. 'Come and join us—it's fun!'

'I don't think we should be playing around,' said Willow. She adjusted her crown of flowers, which looked a bit wonky after she had had to swerve to avoid Patch. 'I think we should stop all this swooping up and down and just fly straight to see the fairy-wrens and not risk dropping things.'

She means her garland, thought Maya. *She is so worried about it that we can't have any fun. Why can't we just enjoy flying in the air together? Why do we need to rush? What's the hurry?*

Chapter Three

'Could I try on your garland?' said Maya to Willow as they flew on through the Kingdom of Birds to the land of the fairy-wrens. 'It's giving me an idea for something I could make for my dad and stepmum's wedding anniversary.'

'Um, no, I don't think so,' said Willow quickly. 'It's really just suitable for a fairy princess. Wait! I'll fly down and say hello to the birds-of-paradise down there. It's important, as the princess, that I know how they are.'

Gorgeous birds-of-paradise were dancing to impress their future mates. Their plumage was so bright and wild, it looked like everyone was dressed up for a party. Maya felt a bit hurt with Willow for not letting her try on the garland, but the wild dancing displays distracted her.

Willow flew back looking a bit cross. 'Well, the birds-of-paradise were a bit caught up in themselves, to be honest,' said Willow, as they carried on. 'They weren't paying attention to anything but their dancing.'

Hmm, I don't think they commented on Willow's garland, thought Maya, smiling to herself.

'Look!' said Patch, his magpie eyes shining with interest. 'We're nearly at the land of the fairy-wrens now! Just look at that new brilliant field of sparkling flowers they have! I've never seen that before!'

Pink and purple and yellow flowers twinkled and flashed as the sun shone on them.

'But why can't we hear or see any fairy-wrens?' said Willow, suddenly sounding a bit worried. 'Normally they sing as they forage for insects together.'

They flew down and landed on the ground and Maya slid off Patch's back, leaning on her sticks.

It was a beautiful place, with pretty flowering trees and shrubs around a little clearing, but the flowers on the shrubs and trees were nothing compared to the spectacular sparkling flowers in the field.

'Look at those shiny petals!' said Patch dreamily, as he hopped towards the flowers. But as soon as his beak touched a gleaming yellow flower he suddenly disappeared in a cloud of glittering stars.

Then the cloud itself vanished, and Patch was nowhere to be seen.

'Patch!' cried Maya, 'Where are you?' and she moved towards the plant. She was just about to stretch out her hand to touch it when—

'No! Keep away!' came a chorus of voices.

Maya and Willow turned around to see Indigo the fairy-wren fairy. He had beautifully-coloured blue wings, and a warm chestnut brown tunic. His hair was short and spiky and he had a sparkling ear stud. He had lots of little brown fairy-wrens around him, but only one blue fairy-wren male. They all looked very jittery and frightened.

'The field of flowers appeared overnight. Most of the superb and splendid fairy-wrens rushed over to pick the petals for their display, but they all vanished at once, like Patch,' said Indigo.

'It's my first time going blue,' said the small blue male, 'but now I'm scared to pick any yellow petals in case I disappear too.'

'Don't pick petals just for me,' said a little brown fairy-wren, shyly. 'I don't want to lose you, Larkspur,' and she touched her bill to his.

'Nonsense!' said an older brown female. 'We can't have wrens pairing up without the petal ceremony. It's our tradition, and we won't break up a tradition whatever Lord Astor says!'

'We've looked everywhere for my daddy, but he's gone,' said one little brown boy wren. 'Lord Astor has taken him!' and he burst into tears. A little brown wren put her wing around him and started crying too.

'Don't worry, Teddy and Hazel,' said

Indigo, and gave the two sobbing little birds a big hug.

'Astor? I knew he must be at the bottom of this,' said Willow, frowning.

'What happened?' said Maya.

'He saw my superb daddy with his beautiful blue feathers, giving my mummy lots of lovely yellow petals,' said the little brown boy wren called Teddy, 'and he asked him why. My daddy said it was because she was so special, the most special person for him in the whole of the Kingdom of Birds, and he loved her. Lord Astor got very cross and said that he was more special than my mummy, and that my daddy should love him and give him yellow flowers too.'

'What did your daddy say to that?' said Princess Willow.

'He said that he didn't love Lord Astor, he loved me,' said Hazel, her voice wobbly but proud. 'He said he wouldn't give him yellow petals, and if he ever gave petals to anyone apart from me, it would be to Princess Willow, the real ruler of the Kingdom of Birds.'

'What did Astor do then?' asked Willow.

'He was very upset and angry,' said

Indigo. 'He summoned me and said that the petal ceremony was banned from now on. I said he didn't have the right to stop it, but he shook his fist and said, "I'll pay you and your fairy-wrens back, just you wait," and flew back to the castle. Then, overnight, the beautiful field of flowers appeared. I was worried there was bad magic but before I could stop them, all the superb males and their splendid cousins flew to pick the petals. And as soon as they touched the flowers they vanished, just like Patch.'

'Except me; I was late,' said the young

blue male, sounding ashamed.

'I'm glad I was able to warn you when you arrived, Larkspur,' said the young brown female.

A little brown girl wren sidled up to Maya and looked at her satchel. She fluttered up into the air and carefully, using her beak, lifted the flap to peek inside.

'Are you the Keeper of the Book?' said the tiny wren in a high clear voice.

There was a murmur of interest from the other wrens.

'Yes, yes I am,' said Maya.

'The Keeper of the Book helps birds,' said the tiny wren. 'When I was a little bird in the nest, Isobel, my big sister, sang me stories at night about you, when she and my brothers and sisters brought me food.'

'I couldn't have laid more eggs this year if my sons and daughters and sister hadn't stayed and brought caterpillars and grasshoppers to the babies,' said Hazel, proudly. 'Even my little Teddy helped.'

'I'm sure Lord Astor is jealous of the fairy-wrens,' said Indigo. 'He doesn't have a happy family.'

'He could have a happy family, if only he would try,' said Willow, sadly.

'Shall I look in the book and see if it can tell us where Patch and the fairy-wrens have gone?' suggested Maya.

'The book!' tweeted the fairy-wrens excitedly, and all hopped over and fluttered around Maya, pressing round her in a feathery crowd.

Maya nervously opened the book and breathed a sigh of relief when she saw the new picture, even though all the fairy-wrens tweeted in distress when they saw it.

There was a big cage of fairy-wrens in a castle room, and with them was Patch, looking very cross.

'Oh no! That's my dear Splendid Sky!' chirped one.

'And my Superb Sapphire,' chirped Teddy's mother, Hazel.

'Daddy!' cried Teddy.

'Where is it?' said Maya to Willow.

'I can see all the glass cases full of royal coronets and necklaces and rings. It's the jewel room in the castle,' said the Princess. 'I used to love looking at all the beautiful jewels and precious stones and gold and silver jewellery. My mother's engagement ring is there. Astor must have put the fairy-wrens in the cage to punish them and stop them giving petals to the females, and he is keeping hold of Patch there to hurt me, because I love him. If Astor isn't the most special person for everybody, he doesn't want anyone else to be. We've just got to get to the castle to get them out, and I'm sure Maya and the book will show us what to do when we get there.'

'But how?' said Maya. 'I can't fly and Patch is in the castle. All of you are too small to carry me.'

'I've got an idea,' said the small brown female fairy-wren. 'Fairy-wrens may be tiny, but we all know how to work together. I'll just go and talk to Indigo. Wait and see.'

Chapter Four

'That's my big sister, Isobel,' said the littlest fairy-wren proudly to Maya. 'She has brilliant ideas. My mum says she will be very good at building nests when she grows up.'

'That's good,' said Maya, smiling at her. 'What is your name?'

'Nell,' whispered the little wren back.

'Well, Isobel has had a great idea,' said Indigo, flying back to tell them. 'One fairy-wren can't carry Maya the way that Patch can, but if they all work together, then we can do it. We need every fairy-wren to fly off and come back with a long vine or creeper.'

'I'll come with you and check you have chosen the right ones,' said Isobel.

Indigo flew to a tree and picked the largest leaf he could and carried it back down to them.

'This is going to be your seat,' said Indigo to Maya.

'How is that going to help me fly?' said Maya. 'Even if a fairy-wren goes on each end, they still won't be strong enough to carry me to the castle.'

'Don't worry. Isobel has thought of that,' said Indigo. 'Now, Nell,' he said to the little fairy-wren. 'Isobel says you will be good at pecking a row of little holes all around the edge of this leaf. Do you think you can do that?'

'Yes,' said Nell, very solemnly, and carefully pecked holes all around the edge.

'I'd love a fairy-wren hole puncher,'

thought Maya. 'But what are they doing?'

Isobel and Larkspur and the other fairy-wrens flew back with lots of trailing creepers.

'Give each strand to Indigo,' said Isobel to the other fairy-wrens. Larkspur gave his strand to Indigo, who attached one end to the leaf by threading it through the hole and tying a knot in the end, and gave the other end back to Larkspur to hold in his beak.

'Can we help?' said Willow, and she and Maya copied Indigo so that the leaf was surrounded by radiating lines, each one's end held by a fairy-wren.

'Now fly up!' said Isobel, 'But hover when we tell you,' and all the fairy-wrens holding creepers flew into the air, bringing the leaf seat up with them.

'Stop!' said Indigo. 'Now, Maya, try to sit down.' Maya sat down on the leaf and brought her legs up so that she was on a little green platform, her sticks beside her, her satchel still over her shoulders. She was suspended in the air by lots of tiny fluttering brown birds and one bright blue one.

Willow clapped her hands with delight. 'Well done, Isobel and Indigo!'

'And you too, Nell,' said Maya to the little wren hopping around with excitement below her.

'Everyone OK?' said Isobel, flying around to check that no bird felt they were carrying too much weight. The fairy-wrens nodded, careful not to let the creepers drop.

'Then off we go to the castle!' said Indigo.

'Follow me!' said Willow, leading the way. Isobel and Indigo flew around the cloud of birds checking each bird was keeping to the same speed. It was important that the platform stayed flat and Maya wasn't tipped out. At first it was a little shaky, but Isobel and Indigo did a great job keeping everyone steady, and Maya could relax.

It was fun being carried by a cloud of birds, over trees, and strange hearing the fluttering of lots of little wings instead of the strong beats of Patch's powerful ones. Those fairy-wrens who weren't holding creepers flew beside them in an anxious twittering crowd, talking about Lord Astor and what was happening to the males and Patch.

'I miss him so much. Poor Patch, stuck in that horrible cage. We've just got to get him out,' Maya said.

'Can we come and sit with you?' panted Nell and the little brown boy fairy-wren, flying beside her. 'We are getting tired flying.'

'Of course,' said Maya, and the two

little wrens came in and sat beside her. They were so light and small they hardly added any extra weight to the leaf.

'This is Teddy,' said Nell, proudly. 'He likes cuddling up next to me. We fairy-wrens all like sitting close to each other.'

Maya thought what sweet little birds the fairy-wrens were and how well they lived together. She looked up to see the mothers and aunts and sisters above them, frowning with concentration as they flew.

'It isn't too far,' said Indigo, flying next to them. 'Look, we can see the castle from here—but I'm a bit worried, as fairy-wrens aren't that good at flying long distances. They are getting tired.'

Maya could feel the leaf tipping a little as one or two birds got weary holding their creeper. It was scary looking down and seeing how far she had to fall. The castle was in sight but they were flying over a lake.

'I can swim,' said Maya to herself, 'but I'd rather not fall in from such a height.'

'This isn't good,' said Isobel, worrying.

Willow flew back.

'What's happening?' she said. 'You're falling behind.'

'We're nearly there,' said Indigo, 'but the fairy-wrens are losing power. They never fly long distances normally.'

'I'll sing my nest song to cheer them up,' said Nell.

'The Keeper of the Book will come
And save the fairy-wrens.
The feathered cloak will be re-made
And Willow rule again.'

It was a catchy tune, and Maya and Indigo and Isobel and Teddy and the other birds all joined in. It seemed to give the birds carrying the leaf the energy they needed, and, to Maya's relief, they managed to cross the lake and land just inside the castle grounds near some shrubs. As soon as they landed the little birds collapsed.

'Thank you so much, brave fairy-wrens,' said Willow. 'Please, take shelter in the shrubs and do not worry, we will rescue Patch and your brothers and husbands and sons.'

Most of the little wrens flew into the shrubs and sat next to each other on the branches inside. They were exhausted.

'But how can we rescue them, Princess Willow?' said Indigo.

'Let's look in the book,' said Teddy and Nell excitedly, still sitting next to Maya on the leaf on the ground.

Maya opened the satchel and took out

the book. There was still just the picture of the jewel room and the cage, but this time a red pencil jumped out of the bag into her hand, and Maya found herself guided to colour in a cloak hanging up on the wall by the cage.

'That's just one of my red silk cloaks,' said Willow. 'I wear it on special occasions, like summer garden parties. That won't unlock any cage. I wonder why the book wants you to notice it?'

'What could it mean?' wondered Maya, as Indigo helped her up from the leaf and handed her her sticks.

'I know where the jewel room is,' said Willow. 'It's on the ground floor, but it is normally guarded, and Astor might be in there with Patch and the fairy-wrens.'

'So we need to distract Lord Astor and the guards so that the jewel room is unattended. Then we need to let Patch and the others out of the cage,' said Maya. 'And the book has pointed us to a big red cloak. Hmm, let me think…' She leant on her sticks for a moment, concentrating, then a big smile spread over her face.

'Larkspur and Isobel!' she said, and

the small blue and the small brown bird each fluttered forward. 'How are you at acting?' she asked. 'I've got two important parts for you to play. I'll tell you and Willow and Indigo what to do in a minute.'

'What about us!' said Teddy and Nell excitedly.

'Don't worry—I have a VERY important job for you two!' said Maya. 'You've got two beaks and I need you to use them. I'll explain to everyone what the plan is, and then you have got to come with me. We've got a rescue to do!'

Chapter Five

'It's just around the corner,' said Willow, and Maya, Indigo, Teddy, Nell, Larkspur, and Isobel followed her until they were just under the window of the jewel room. They could hear Lord Astor's angry voice.

'If you won't admit that I am the most important person in the Kingdom of

Birds, then you can stay in there and rot.'

His voice changed again, and got more friendly.

'Look—you're smart birds, you look good. I like your blue feathers. I like your style. If you'd only present me with coloured petals and show the rest of the Kingdom of Birds how much you love me, you can be my right-hand birds, my closest friends. If you love me, then I will love you. It's as simple as that.'

'They don't love you. It's as simple as that,' came Patch's voice.

'Shut up, Magpie. Who asked you?'

snapped Lord Astor. 'They say you corvids are so clever, but you aren't. You refused to be my deputy, so you are not the smart birds you think you are, and that's a fact.'

'I will only ever serve Princess Willow, and that's a fact,' retorted Patch. 'And no magpie, rook, crow, raven, jay, or any other members of the EXTREMELY clever corvid family would say differently.'

'And we fairy-wrens agree!' came another voice.

'That's my daddy,' whispered Teddy, proudly.

Maya nodded at Willow. Willow nodded back.

'Here goes,' she said, and flew around the corner.

'Lord Astor! Lord Astor! It's Princess Willow!' shouted the guards.

'After her, you fools!' shouted Lord Astor. 'I'll deal with you later,' he snarled.

Maya peered round the corner and saw Willow flying off, with Lord Astor and the guards in hot pursuit.

'Now go, Indigo,' she said, and Indigo flew into the jewel room and was back around the corner with the long red silk cloak. He laid it on the ground next to Maya.

'Indigo? What's going on?' called out Patch and the fairy-wrens.

'Ssh—Maya will explain in a minute,' called Indigo.

He helped Maya kneel down next to the cloak. She got out a pencil and quickly made some pencil marks on the cloth.

'Right, I've traced the lines you two need to peck along,' said Maya to Nell and Teddy. 'First a circle, then a spiral inside. Get going!' The two little birds started pecking lots of tiny little holes along the pencil marks.

'Patch,' called Maya. 'We're here to rescue you all, but nobody must let Lord Astor know we are here. When he catches and brings Willow in don't worry, but act upset. Carry on arguing with him as normal.'

'That will be a pleasure,' called out Patch, grimly.

'We've finished!' said Nell and Teddy.

'Quick,' said Maya to Indigo. 'Carefully tear the silk along the pecked line of holes Nell and Teddy have made.'

Indigo carefully tore the silk so that
they had a long red spiral.

Maya leant against the wall and took one of her sticks.

'Give the cloth spiral to me,' she said, and carefully wound the cloth around the stick so that it looked like a huge red rose. It was a very big version of the ones she had made with Theo and Saffron. She held the flower at the bottom and slid the stick out.

'Now take the end in your beak, Larkspur,' she said. 'Hold it tight. Indigo and Isobel, you know what to do? Fly a distance away from the room so Lord Astor has to leave it to see you. You are going to have to say everything, because if Larkspur opens his beak to speak the flower will unravel.'

The others, safely out of sight in their hiding place around the corner, heard the sound of people returning. Maya's heart was beating fast—would her plan succeed? It had to—or poor Willow would be Lord Astor's captive too!

'Well, well, well, what have we here?' sneered Lord Astor from inside the jewel room. 'My meddling niece. The one everybody loves so much.'

'Oh no! You've got Princess Willow!'

said Patch. He was a very good actor.

'Let Patch and the fairy-wrens go!' said Willow.

'No,' said Lord Astor. 'And you're going in the cage with them.'

'At least they are loyal to me, not like that awful Larkspur the fairy-wren' said Willow. 'He is insisting on presenting you with the biggest flower in the kingdom. The traitor. He is flying here now. I came here to stop him giving it to you.'

'Larkspur?' said Teddy's father's shocked voice. 'My nephew? I can't believe it!'

'The biggest flower in the kingdom?' said Lord Astor, delightedly. 'Where is it? Where is this superb fairy-wren? At last someone sees sense.'

Suddenly there was a big commotion. Out at the far end of the garden was a bright blue fairy-wren holding a most enormous red rose in his beak, being shouted at by two little brown birds and a blue-winged fairy. Larkspur and Isobel and Indigo were playing their parts to perfection.

'You wicked fairy-wren!' shouted Isobel, so loudly and clearly everyone could hear. 'When your feathers turned blue you said you would give ME petals. Now you want to give the best flower in the kingdom to that horrible Lord Astor.'

'You shouldn't give Lord Astor ANYTHING!' yelled Nell. 'If you don't want to give my sister that rose you should give it to Princess Willow.'

'As the fairy-wren guardian I absolutely forbid you to do this!' proclaimed Indigo.

'It's no good,' shouted Isobel to Indigo, 'He is insisting on presenting it to Lord Astor, here out in the garden.'

'At last—someone who values me,' said

Lord Astor flying out of the room. 'Come, guards, see how a truly loyal bird treats me. Bring Princess Willow so she can see it for herself.'

As soon as Lord Astor and the guards and Willow left, Teddy and Nell rushed into the room, Maya following as fast as she could.

'Quick! We have got to find the keys! We don't have much time!' said Maya.

'Am I pleased to see you!' said Patch.

'Do you know where the keys are kept?' said Maya, desperately opening all the drawers she could find and looking on the back of the door for hooks. There were no keys to be seen, and little Teddy and Nell were flying round and round in panicked circles, tiring themselves out, and not finding anything.

'Oh dear,' thought Maya 'They are still baby birds and maybe this is too difficult for them.'

'Look up!' said Patch.

A bunch of golden keys was high up on a hook.

Of course, thought Maya, *fairies can fly so they can keep keys right up by the ceiling.* 'Nell, Teddy, can you fly up and get them?'

'I'll go!' tweeted both little birds, but in their excitement they flew right into each other and bumped heads.

'Ouch!' they both said, but bravely kept flying up.

'I can't do it. I'm sorry!' panted tiny Teddy, and fluttered down to the ground.

Nell managed to fly up as high as the keys, but try as she might she couldn't get them off the hook.

'I'm sorry. They are too heavy for me,' she panted, and tumbled rather than flew down to the ground to sit breathless next to her little friend. 'Oh Maya, what are we going to do?'

'Think like a corvid!' called Patch. 'We magpies use sticks to get things.'

'Brilliant, Patch!' said Maya. She saw some brocade on the curtains and quickly pulled it off. Leaning against one of the glass cases to keep her balance, she used the brocade to tightly lash one of her sticks tightly against the other, to make one long stick. Then she used the top of this new super-long stick to unhook the keys so they fell with a clatter to the floor.

'Hooray!' cheered Teddy and Nell.

Maya used the extended stick to skilfully hook them again and drag them towards her. Finally they were in her hands! She quickly untied the brocade so she had two normal-sized sticks again, and was unlocking the cage in no time.

'Thank you, Maya!' said Patch, 'I was so squashed in there,' and Maya flung her arms around him as he put his head on her shoulder. It was so lovely to hug him again.

'Daddy!' cried Teddy to a particularly magnificent blue bird.

'My son!' the blue bird said proudly.

'Fly, fairy-wrens!' Maya called, and they all flew out of the open door in a blue cloud.

But suddenly Lord Astor was back in the room with his guards, holding a ripped up red silk cloak in his hands, and looking furious. They were blocking the exit—Patch and Maya were trapped.

'How dare you let the fairy-wrens escape!' Lord Astor said to Maya angrily. 'You meddling human child. I suppose you have something to do with this pretend flower . . .' and he threw the ripped silk cloak at her in disgust.

'All I ever really wanted was for the fairy-wrens to love me,' he whined, self-pityingly.

'You can't make anyone love you,' said Maya. 'If you loved the fairy-wrens first, and let them give each other petals, if you had been kind and generous, then they would have loved you too. But whilst you are mean and selfish, and rule a stolen kingdom instead of Princess Willow, nobody will love you.'

'Rubbish!' snarled Lord Astor. 'You have spoilt everything. Guards—seize the girl and the magpie and put them in the cage. And take that bag off her first. I want that book!'

'No!' shouted Maya. 'You will never have the book!'

Patch bravely stood in front of her, his cramped wings outstretched, ready to fight the advancing guards as Lord Astor threw back his head and laughed an evil laugh.

'You'll never escape now!' he said.

Then suddenly the room was filled with hundreds of tiny blue and brown birds and a furious Princess Willow and Indigo.

'Take that, you wicked Uncle!' shouted Princess Willow, and grabbing her beloved spring crown from her head she shoved it on Lord Astor's head and over his eyes so he couldn't see. A cloud of fairy-wrens flew around the guards to confuse them, and they all managed to push Lord Astor and his guards into the cage and lock them in.

'I'm sure the other guards will come and let you out soon,' said Willow, 'but I hope you have some time in there to think about how horrible you are being, Uncle. Fairies and birds have always lived in harmony and peace in this kingdom and my father never ruled the way you are—you should be ashamed of yourself.'

'Never!' said Lord Astor, shaking his fist. Indigo and Willow quickly lifted Maya back on to Patch's back and they all flew out and away from the castle.

Chapter
Six

Indigo could quickly see that Patch was really struggling to fly with Maya on his back. His wings were cramped after being locked in the cage.

'Let's fly down and pick up the leaf harness,' Indigo said. 'Maya can come back to the land of the fairy-wrens the same way she came. That will give Patch a chance to recover and stretch his wings after being in the cage.'

So Willow took off Patch's riding harness and gave it to Indigo to carry.

'I'll carry the satchel and quiver of sticks to take some weight off you,' she said, taking them. Maya noticed that Willow was looking a little sad, and remembered how Willow had taken off her beautiful spring garland and used it to save her. That was a really big thing for her to do. She had been so proud of it.

The blue fairy-wrens all wanted to

carry Maya, to thank her for saving them, so Maya sat back and enjoyed flying under a feathery blue cloud. This time, to stop the fairy-wrens getting tired, they took it in turns to hold the strings, and Indigo and Isobel flew around and made sure that the transfer of strings from beak to beak went smoothly. Teddy and Nell sat next to Maya and chatted to her and made her laugh, and in no time at all they had arrived back at the land of the fairy-wrens and landed on the green grass.

The sparkling flowers had disappeared as mysteriously as they had appeared, but the gardens were full of beautiful flowering shrubs, and as soon as they arrived, the blue fairy-wrens were off picking petals and presenting them to their mates. It was such a happy scene.

Maya looked over at Willow, sadly patting her hair, and had an idea. Nell and Teddy flew off and chose some lovely flowers from the bushes, then helped Maya find little stalks to string them together.

'Willow—this is for you,' she called, and Willow turned round.

'Oh, Maya! Thank you! It's so beautiful!' she said, as Maya put a new, even lovelier garland on her friend's curls.

'And Indigo and Patch—come here!' said Maya. She had made two smaller garlands for them to wear. Indigo was delighted but Patch pretended he wasn't.

'I look ridiculous!' said Patch, but he didn't try to take it off, and Maya noticed him strutting around rather proudly and trying to catch sight of his reflection in a little garden pool.

'Princess Willow, we know that you are gathering feathers for the cloak,' said Teddy's daddy, the most magnificent blue splendid fairy-wren. 'On behalf of all the fairy-wrens, I would like to present you with one of mine.'

He laid a beautiful blue feather at Willow's feet.

'Thank you so much!' said Princess Willow, and then looked a little sadly over at Maya.

'Dear Maya, you know this means our time together is ended for now. Please put this feather in your book and take it to your world for safe-keeping.'

Patch and Willow and Maya gave each other a big hug.

'Thank you for saving us, just like the song said,' chirped Nell and Teddy.

'Thank you for bringing us back

together,' said Isobel and Larkspur. Isobel had a big pile of yellow petals at her feet, and was looking very pleased.

'It's been lovely getting to know you all,' said Maya to the loving little fairy-wren families, and she placed the feather on a blank page in the book. All at once the feather began to glow, and Maya was surrounded by a cloud of glittering, swirling feathers again, and when they cleared she found herself back in her room, sitting at her desk. Her satchel was back in its position over her chair, and the book was open in front of her, with a magically-coloured-in scene of happy blue fairy-wrens picking yellow and pink and purple flowers. In the corner was the fairy-wren feather, magically changed into a drawing until all the feathers for the cloak had been gathered.

Maya had no time to feel sad. There was a gentle tapping on the door.

'Come in!' she said, and suddenly there was her lovely big sister, Lauren, giving her a hug. It was so good to see her again.

'Hello Maya!' said Lauren. 'I've got the food for the special meal. What's that pile of coloured paper doing on your desk!'

'I've got an idea about that!' said Maya.

'Thank you so much, girls,' said Penny happily. 'I don't remember ever having had such a delicious anniversary meal! The room looks so beautiful decorated with all those paper flowers, and I have never seen your father looking so smart!'

Maya laughed. 'I think a red tie and a blue shirt look good on Dad,' she said.

'And the yellow roses you gave me are beautiful, darling,' Penny said to Maya's dad.

'Maya helped me choose them,' he said. 'She said they matched my shirt! I must say, I've never chosen the colour of your flowers for that reason before. The only thing I'm not sure about are the flower garlands she made us all wear— you look good, but I'm not sure about me.'

'You know you look great, Dad,' laughed Lauren. 'I saw you glancing in the mirror!'

Maya smiled. She had made garlands for Theo and Saffron too, and she couldn't wait to give them to them. *I know why Larkspur feels so happy giving petals to Isobel,* she thought. *When you love someone you want* to do special things for them and spend time with them. I love my family and my friends, and I love how the fairy-wrens love each other. It was so wonderful meeting them. I wonder which birds will need our help next time in the Magical Kingdom of Birds?

Acknowledgements

I have really enjoyed learning facts about
fairy-wrens from reading about them and
watching videos online. What amazing
characters fairy-wrens are, and how lucky
we are to have them in our world!

Thank you to my friend Helen Sole, play
therapist, teacher and sitting volleyball athlete,
for advice on Maya's problems with her legs.

Thank you to my lovely agent, Anne Clark,
and to Liz Cross, Debbie Sims and Clare
Whitston from OUP for all their enthusiasm
for this series. Thank you to Fraser Hutchinson
and Hannah Penny and all who work in Trade
Marketing and Publicity for all your support.

Thank you to Rosie Butcher for her wonderful illustrations and for Lizzie Smart the designer for making this book, like all the others, look so gorgeous.

Thank you to my lovely neighbours, the Haynes family, for being so supportive of all my books, and I hope that Theo and Saffron and Emma enjoy seeing their names in this book!

Thank you to my children Joanna, Michael, Laura and Christina for their support, and my lovely husband Graeme, who often wears a red tie with a blue shirt, and gives me flowers, and chocolate, and lots of love.

About Anne

Every Christmas, Anne used to ask for a dog. She had to wait many years, but now she has two dogs, called Timmy and Ben. Timmy is a big, gentle golden retriever who loves people and food and is scared of cats. Ben is a small brown and white cavalier King Charles spaniel who is a bit like a cat because he curls up in the warmest places and bosses Timmy about. He snuffles and snorts quite a lot, and you can tell what he is feeling by the way he walks. He has a particularly pleased patter when he has stolen something he shouldn't have, which gives him away immediately. Anne lives in a village in Kent and is not afraid of spiders.

About Rosie

Rosie lives in a little town in East Yorkshire with her husband and daughter. She draws and paints by night, but by day she builds dens on the sofa, watches films about princesses, and attends tea parties. Rosie enjoys walking and having long conversations with her little girl, Penelope. They usually discuss important things like spider webs, birds, and prickly leaves.

Bird Fact File

Turn the page for information
on the real-life birds that
inspired this story.

Fun Facts

Find out all about these superb
and splendid birds

1. There are eleven species of fairy-wren,
including the splendid fairy-wren and the
superb fairy-wren.

2. Fairy-wrens grow about 14 cm long, which
includes their 6 cm long tail!

3. Their long tail helps them to balance. It is
usually held upright and is rarely still.

4. Male fairy-wrens change colour every year, from dull brown to bright blue.

5. Male fairy-wrens pluck flower petals and display them to females as part of a courtship display. Splendid fairy-wrens mostly choose pink or purple petals to contrast with their feathers, and superb fairy-wrens mostly choose yellow petals.

6. Fairy-wrens have fairly weak powers of flight so spend most of their time on the ground or in shrubs, progressing in a series of hops.

7. Fairy-wrens eat mainly insects, and sometimes seeds.

8. Fairy-wrens like to sing while they forage for food.

9. They forage in a group, with insects disturbed by one bird often eaten by another.

10. The group shelters and rests together during the heat of the day.

11. Fairy-wrens listen to the warning cries of other birds to avoid danger.

12. Nest building is done entirely by the female, using spiders' webs, fine twigs, and grass.

13. Fairy-wrens build their nests about 1 metre off the ground, under cover of shrubs.

14. Fairy-wrens live in small groups, who all help to raise the three or four chicks that are laid every brood.

15. The mother is the only bird to sit on the nest and incubate the eggs, but all members of the group feed the chicks.

16. The mothers sing a special 'nest song' to the chicks when they are still inside their eggs, and the rest of the family learn it too!

Where do you find fairy-wrens?

The only place that you can find fairy-wrens living in the wild is in Australia!

Turn the page for some fantastic

Bird activities

Make an egg-cellent fairy-wren by decorating an egg!

You will need:

- Fresh eggs in an egg box
- A drawing pin
- A cocktail stick
- A straw
- A small bowl
- A kebab skewer
- Blue paint
- A sponge
- Blue craft feathers
- A marker pen
- Paper
- Glue

First you will need to blow your egg, to get rid of the insides. Why not use them to have an omelette for lunch afterwards?

1. Using the egg box to keep it steady, carefully push a hole in the top of your egg with the drawing pin. Use the pin to make the hole a big bigger.

2. Insert the cocktail stick to widen the hole a bit more, and stir it around inside the egg to break up the yolk.

3. Repeat steps 1 and 2 on the bottom of the egg. Try and make the hole on the bottom a bit bigger if you can, but be careful not to crack the shell.

4. Hold your egg over the bowl, place the straw over the hole at the top, and blow!

5. Blow through the straw until all the egg's insides have come out into the bowl, and you are left with just the shell.

6. Wash the egg shell under the kitchen tap, then leave to dry.

Now you're ready to turn your shell into a beautiful fairy-wren!

1. Stick a kebab skewer in the bottom hole of your egg and stand it in a cup – this will make it easier to paint.

2. Sponge the blue paint all over your egg and then leave to dry.

3. Take your blue craft feathers, and poke one through the hole at the back of your egg, making a nice long tail.

4. Stick a feather to each side of your egg to make wings.

5. For its eyes, cut two small circles out of white paper and draw a black dot in the middle. Glue these on to the front of your egg.

6. Fold a yellow piece of paper in half, cut it in a triangle shape, and your bird has a beak! Carefully glue the folded end on to the front of your egg. Superb!

Make a beautiful paper flower, just like Maya and her friends in the story!

You will need:

- Coloured paper (make sure it is coloured on both sides)
- Pipe cleaners
- Scissors
- Large cup to draw around
- A pencil
- Sticky tape

Step 1

Draw around the cup to make a circle on the coloured paper.

Step 2

Using the scissors, cut out the circle.

Step 3

Starting from the outside, cut a spiral in the circle.

Step 4

Tape the pipe cleaner to the outside end of the spiral, and start wrapping the paper around and around.

Step 5

Let the paper unravel a little if you want a fuller bloom.

Step 6

Secure the end of the spiral with a small piece of sticky tape.

Step 7

Repeat! Why not cut the spiral thinner or thicker to make different types of roses?

Make a brilliant bottle birdfeeder!

Welcome the birds into your garden with this creative and tasty snack that will leave them wanting a return visit.

Make sure you have an adult to help you!

You will need:

- A clear bottle
- Two pencils or skewers
- Scissors
- Birdseed
- String

Step 1

Getting an adult to help you, use scissors to make two little holes opposite each other towards the bottom of the bottle. These holes should be the size of the pencils or skewers you are using. Then, poke the pencil/skewer through the holes so that it is poking out a bit on each side.

Step 2

Do the same on the other side of the bottle, so that the pencils/skewers make a cross. This is where the birds will perch while they are eating the tasty birdseed.

Step 3

Use the scissors to cut a small hole above all four of the perches. This hole needs to be big enough for the birds to get to the seed, but not so big that the seeds fall out easily.

Step 4

Take your birdseed and fill up the bottle all the way to the top.

Step 5

Put the lid on
the bottle.

Step 6

Tie your string around the neck
of the bottle and tie the other
end onto a strong tree branch in
your garden.

Now you have made a place for all the birds
to have a tasty snack to return to whenever
they are hungry, and you can watch it all
from your window!

Join Maya for another adventure in
The Ice Swans

The Magical Kingdom of Birds is in trouble! Wicked Lord Astor has frozen Swan Lake and turned its beautiful swans into statues. Can Maya, with the help of her friends, Willow and Patch, break the enchantment and save the day?

Magical kingdom of Birds

The Ice Swans

ANNE BOOTH

Illustrated by Rosie Butcher

Chapter One

'Maya—don't forget to get ready for skating!' Penny called from the kitchen. 'You'll need a warm coat and hat and gloves, for the outside rink.'

It was Saturday afternoon, when normally Maya and her big sister, Lauren, would do things together. Lauren had gone away to university now, though, and

Maya's dad and stepmum, Penny, were taking her out for a special treat. The trouble was, Maya didn't want to go.

'I'll never be able to ice skate,' said Maya to her dad in the hallway, knowing Penny couldn't hear. 'I know Penny loved it when she was my age, but she didn't have problems with her legs, like I do. I know I'll just look silly. I'll hate it and I won't be any good, so what's the point?'

'Don't say that, love,' said her dad. 'Look at how good you have got at riding.'

But Maya wasn't listening to him. 'Why did Penny sign me up for those stupid lessons anyway?' she grumbled, pulling on her hat.

'She's worried you are missing your big sister. Penny thought ice skating would be something fun you could do together,' said Dad.

'Are you ready, Maya?' said Penny, coming into the hall. 'Where are your gloves?'

'In my room, I think. I'll go and get them,' said Maya.

'Be quick!' called Penny. 'My friend can't wait to meet you. She is such a great teacher, she'll have you whizzing round the ice rink in no time at all. It's going to be such fun!'

'For you, maybe, not for me,' said Maya under her breath, as she went into her room.

She didn't mean to slam the door quite so hard behind her, but it crashed shut and the satchel on the back of the door fell off. Some pencils and a large book fell out and rolled across the floor.

'Oh no,' said Maya. She managed to pick up the colouring pencils and put them back into the satchel. Then she picked up the book and carried it over to

the table by the window to check it hadn't

been damaged.

'I'm so sorry,' she said to the book. It

was an extraordinarily beautiful book,

covered in deep-blue cloth with tiny shimmering golden pictures of all sorts of birds. The book itself seemed to glow and tingle in her hands as she spoke to it, and Maya felt her heart beat a little faster. Maybe it was time. Maybe the book hadn't fallen out because she had slammed the door. Maybe it had fallen out because today, at last, she would be allowed back into the Kingdom of Birds. She had already had one adventure in the kingdom and she knew there were more waiting for her, but she couldn't go back unless the book showed her a magic picture to colour in.

'I'd much rather be riding Patch the Magpie than looking silly falling over on the ice,' said Maya, as she picked up her purple woollen gloves and pulled them on. 'I'm the Keeper of the Book, after all, and I need to get back to help Princess Willow regain her kingdom.' She glanced out of the window, and suddenly she saw a big black and white bird fly into the garden. It was a magpie, and it swooped low over the grass and landed just near the window. It tilted its head, its black eyes shining, and seemed to Maya to give her a nod.

My friends must be ready for me, she thought and, taking a deep breath, she opened the book. *Please, magic book, let there be a picture this time.*

Maya had looked in the book every day since she last visited the kingdom, but the pages had been blank. This time, however, she was not disappointed. The book fell open to a picture of an icy tower on a frozen lake. The tower was surrounded by ice sculptures of swans—some big, some very little.

Maya grabbed an ice-blue pencil and began to shade in the tower. She could feel that something incredible was about to happen. Suddenly, all she could see in front of her were whirling, glittering, sparkling, white and black feathers, and a cloud of glittering snow. This was how she had entered the Kingdom of Birds the first time, so she wasn't scared when she was lifted up into the air, and started falling into the picture she had been colouring; tumbling and spinning down into the sparkling magic.

More magic awaits

Magical kingdom
of Birds
The Missing Fairy-Wrens

ANNE BOOTH
Illustrated by Rosie Butcher

OUT
SOON!

Magical kingdom
of Birds
The Silent Songbirds

ANNE BOOTH
Illustrated by Rosie Butcher

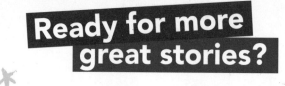